ABOUT THE BOOK

Hattie was having a birthday, and for the first time she was allowed to invite her own friends to her party. She decided to include Edward, the new boy who had just moved to her street. She thought he was cute. Edward, however, informed her he was coming only for the cake. Knowing he would not like any dumb pink frosting, Hattie asked her mother for catsup icing. When that request was emphatically denied, Hattie "helpfully" takes matters into her own hands in this first of three easy-to-read, delightful stories.

Hattie's attempts to be helpful always have surprising and funny results, and each story is accompanied by charming black-and-white illustrations by Susanna Natti.

HELPFUL HATTIE

A LET ME READ BOOK

by Janet Quin-Harkin

ILLUSTRATED BY

Susanna Natti

HARCOURT BRACE JOVANOVICH, PUBLISHERS
SAN DIEGO   NEW YORK   LONDON

Text copyright © 1983 by Janet Quin-Harkin
Illustrations copyright © 1983 by Susanna Natti

Printed in the United States of America

LIBRARY OF CONGRESS CATALOGING IN PUBLICATION DATA
Quin-Harkin, Janet.
Helpful Hattie.
(A Let me read book)
Summary: Hattie tries to help her mother by
frosting her own birthday cake, cutting her own hair,
and sticking a tooth back into her mouth
for a photograph session,
with rather unusual results.
[1. Birthdays—Fiction. 2. Haircutting—Fiction.
3. Teeth—Fiction. 4. Helpfulness—Fiction] I. Natti,
Susanna, ill. II. Title. III. Series.
PZ7.Q419He 1983   [E]   82-15723
ISBN 0-15-233756-3   ISBN 0-15-233757-1

B   C   D   E   FIRST EDITION   B   C   D   E   (PBK.)

Designed by Barbara DuPree Knowles

CL '84
APR

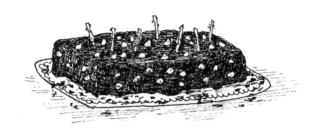

HATTIE AND THE CATSUP CAKE

"Happy birthday to me! Happy birthday to me!" Hattie sang as she rode her bike down the street. "It's my birthday today," she called to Edward.

Edward had just moved to Hattie's street.
He had so many freckles that his face looked
like an orange blob. Hattie thought he was
very cute.

"I know it's your birthday," Edward said. He did not think Hattie was cute at all. Edward did not like girls.

"You're coming to my party," Hattie said happily.

"No, I'm not," said Edward.

"You have to," Hattie said. "I invited you, and your mother said you have to come."

"I'm only coming for the cake," Edward said. "Then I'm going home again. I'm not playing any dumb girl games either."

"See you later, Edward," Hattie yelled as she rode home.

This birthday was very special for Hattie.
She had had birthdays before but never with
her own friends. But this was going to be a
real party. Her own friends were coming.
Even Edward would be there!

When Hattie got home, her mother was
baking.

"What sort of cake would you like this year?" her mother asked.

"A gorilla-shaped one," said Hattie.

"Oh, Hattie, be serious," said her mother. "You know that is not what I meant. What sort of frosting do you want . . . pink, white, chocolate . . . ?"

"Catsup," said Hattie.

"Hattie, you're impossible," said her mother. "You know you can't have catsup frosting. Nobody wants to eat a catsup cake."

"Why don't you have pink to match your new dress?" her mother asked. "Pink would be pretty."

"I want it to be a special party," Hattie said. "I want Edward to like it. I know he won't like dumb pink frosting."

"Boys like anything sweet and sticky," said her mother. "Now let's get dressed."

Hattie wanted to have the best party in the world. She stood still while her mother put her hair into two ponytails. She even put on the new pink dress that Grandmother had sent her.

"You look very nice," her mother said. "Your friends won't know you without your jeans. Now stay clean while I get dressed, and then we will frost the cake together."

Hattie went downstairs and sat on the
piano stool and swung her legs. After a few
swings she said, "Mommie seems to be taking
a long time. The kids will be here soon. I
think I had better *help* Mommie and frost
the cake for her . . ."

When Hattie's mother came downstairs,
she opened her eyes very wide. "Hattie!"
she said. "What have you done to the cake?"

"I frosted it for you," said Hattie. "You took too long."

"What did you frost it with, Hattie?" her mother asked.

Hattie smiled. "With catsup. That's the red. The white is the mayonnaise, and the orange blobs are mustard. Do you like my pretzel candles?"

"Oh, Hattie," said her mother. "What am I going to do? I can't bake another cake before the children come. I'll just have to scrape off this mess."

She grabbed a knife, but before she could scrape off the catsup, the doorbell rang.

Hattie opened the door. In came a whole group of children with presents for Hattie. Edward pushed ahead and looked around the room. Then he saw the cake through the open kitchen door and ran toward it.

"That's a neat-looking cake," he said. "What kind of frosting is that?" Before Hattie's mother could stop him, Edward dipped his finger in the frosting. "Boy!" he shouted. "It's catsup. Catsup frosting!"

The rest of the children then came into the kitchen to hear what was going on.

"We made a mistake," said Hattie's mother quickly. "I will make some real frosting right now. You can have cake later . . ."

"I want my cake right now," said Edward. "I never had catsup frosting."

One little girl said, "Yucchhh!" but the other children all said, "We want to try it right now. We want to try it right now!"

And so, without even having time to put on real candles, Hattie's mother had to cut the cake. Then she had to cut more slices until the cake was all gone.

"Boy," said Edward. "That was the best cake I ever ate. Can you teach my mom to make frosting like that?"

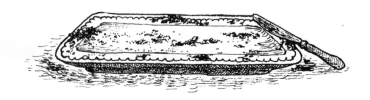

HATTIE AND THE HAIRCUT

"Hattie," said her mother one day, "your
hair is getting too long. I think we should
get it cut."

Hattie did not want to get her hair cut. She liked it long. She liked the way it flew out when she ran. She liked the way it got in her eyes on windy days.

But the worst thing about haircuts was the lady at the beauty shop. She had blue hair. It was piled up on her head in lots of curls. She had a face that scared Hattie. It looked as if it might crack if she ever smiled, but she never smiled anyway. Worst of all, her nails were like birds' claws and scratched Hattie.

Remembering her haircuts in the past, Hattie wondered if the hair lady were a witch in disguise. One thing Hattie was sure of—she did not like little girls!

"Sit still, dear," she would say in a soft, silky voice. "Don't look up, dear." She

sounded sweet and gentle, but her fingers
weren't sweet and gentle at all.

In the end she always said, "Now, doesn't
that look pretty?"

Hattie never thought it did. But Mother
always said, "Yes, very pretty," and paid
the lady.

Now Hattie looked at her hair in the mirror. Then she had a good idea. She would *help* her mother by cutting her own hair. That way she could cut just a little, and she wouldn't have to visit the beauty-shop lady.

She got out the big scissors. Then she went back to the mirror.

"I'll start with the front," she said.
"Mommie doesn't like my hair in my eyes."

She picked up a handful of hair and cut.
There was a loud snipping sound, and pieces
of hair fell down her face.

"There," said Hattie. "That was easy."

She looked at her short hair in the mirror.
"Oh, dear," she said.

The hair she had cut stuck out like
toothbrush bristles. It was much too short.

Just then Mother walked in. She saw
Hattie and stopped in horror.

"I was just putting it back," said Hattie
quickly. She picked up some hair from the rug.

"You can't put it back," her mother cried.

"Not even with glue?" asked Hattie.

"No."

"Not even if I staple it?"

"No."

"Not even with sticky tape?"

At last her mother laughed. "No, not even with tape. And there is no way to hide it. You'll just have to wait for it to grow again."

"But I can't go to school looking like a toothbrush!" Hattie wailed.

"You'll have to."

"But the kids will laugh at me."

"Then you will learn not to do silly things by yourself," said her mother. "But maybe we can buy you a hat . . ."

"A baseball cap?" Hattie asked.

"All right," said Mother, "a baseball cap."

So Hattie went to school wearing a baseball cap. She told the teacher why she didn't want to take it off. Her teacher said she could keep it on all day.

But on the way home from school a bad thing happened. When she was right next to Edward's house, the wind blew. Off came the baseball cap. It landed at Edward's feet.

"Hey, Hattie!" Edward called. "You dropped your cap."

"Thank you," said Hattie. She looked away from him, down the street. She held out her hand behind her.

"What's the matter?" Edward asked.
"Why won't you turn around?"

"I'm in a big hurry," said Hattie. "I'm in
too big a hurry to look back. So please may I
have my cap? Then I can hurry home."

"Here," said Edward. He put the cap into
her hand. "Boy," he said, "you act funny
sometimes."

Hattie put the cap back on her head and
started to run, but the wind snatched it off
again. Hattie tried to catch the flying
cap—and bumped straight into Edward.

"Hattie!" said Edward. "What happened
to your hair?"

Hattie tried to think of all sorts of neat
things to say, but in the end all she said was,
"I cut it. By mistake."

Edward looked at Hattie's hair. Hattie looked at an ant on the sidewalk.

Then Edward said, "I think it looks neat. It's not stupid curls like all those other dumb girls have."

"Where's your cap?" Hattie's mother asked when Hattie came running home.

"I don't need it any more," said Hattie. "Edward says my hair looks neat."

HATTIE AND THE TOOTH

Hattie had a loose tooth. She was very
excited. All the other children in her class
had already lost a tooth. They brought the

teeth to Show and Tell. They showed Hattie the gaps where the old teeth had been. They even showed her the quarters that the tooth fairy had brought.

Mary Ellen Roth, who sat next to Hattie, had lost four teeth.

"How come your teeth don't ever fall out?" Mary Ellen asked Hattie. "You must be a baby."

"I am not," said Hattie. But she was scared in case she never got grown-up teeth—and also that the tooth fairy would never come to her house.

At last a tooth was loose. She could make
it go backward and forward with her tongue.

"I wish it would come out right now," she
told Edward. "I want the tooth fairy to bring
me a quarter."

"The tooth fairy brings me a dollar," said
Edward.

"A whole dollar!!" said Hattie. "I wish I
could make this dumb tooth fall out."

"Why don't you pull it out?" asked Edward.

"By myself?"

"You scared?"

"I'm not scared," said Hattie.

She put her fingers on the tooth and pulled. It hurt. The tooth wiggled but did not come out.

"It won't come," she said.

"You have to pull harder," said Edward.

"You pull it for me," said Hattie.

"Not me," said Edward. "Why don't you tie it to the doorknob?"

"No, thanks," said Hattie.

"Then ask your mom," said Edward, and he ran home.

That night Hattie asked her mother to pull
out the tooth. But her mother said, "The
tooth is not ready yet, Hattie. Just wait and
one day it will fall out by itself, without
anyone's help." So Hattie waited.

The tooth got looser and looser, but it still didn't fall out. It got so wiggly that Hattie could put her tongue under it and make it move from side to side. All the children in her class watched her wiggle her tooth. Then they all screamed, "Eeeuuwww!!!"

Miss Curtis, her teacher, wanted to pull the tooth out for Hattie, but Hattie said, "I mustn't pull the tooth. I promised my mother I wouldn't." So Miss Curtis had to wait.

Then one day it did fall out, right in the middle of math class. Hattie was wiggling it. It gave a funny click and dropped onto her math paper.

"My tooth just fell out," Hattie yelled. All the children jumped in their seats. Miss Curtis dropped her chalk.

"Hattie!" said Miss Curtis. "How often do I have to tell you—when you have something to say, you must raise your hand first."

"But you were looking at the blackboard," said Hattie. "I didn't want to wait for hours with my hand raised. My arm gets tired. I wanted to tell everyone about my tooth."

Miss Curtis smiled. "Well, I suppose a tooth falling out is special, Hattie," she said. "We will take a good look at it later. But now we must finish our math papers quickly. The photographer is coming to take our class picture."

Soon the man came with his camera. Miss Curtis made sure the children looked neat and tidy. "Now line up," said Miss Curtis, "and we shall go out to the front steps."

Mary Ellen Roth looked at Hattie. "You will spoil the whole picture with that big gap in your teeth," said Mary Ellen. "You'll look ugly!"

Hattie stopped in horror. Mary Ellen was the meanest girl in the class, if not the whole world, but she was right. A gap would look ugly. Hattie would be the ugliest girl in the class!

"Move on, Hattie," said Miss Curtis.
"You're holding up the line."

Then Hattie had an idea. She went back,
grabbed her tooth, and took it with her. "I'll
stick it back in for the photo," she said
helpfully. "Then I'll look like everyone else."

On the front steps Miss Curtis made them stand in rows. Hattie put herself in front of Mary Ellen, but Miss Curtis moved her. "You're much taller than Mary Ellen, Hattie," said Miss Curtis. "Let her stand in front of you."

"See," said Mary Ellen. "You're ugly— that's why they want you in back." She stood in front of Hattie and shook out her curly hair.

"Now, I want to see a lot of big smiles," said the photographer. "When I count to three, I want you all to say *cheese.*"

The children giggled—all except Hattie.

She was busy sticking the tooth back into
her mouth.

"Quit wriggling," said Edward.

"I wasn't wriggling," Hattie whispered.

"You were too," said Edward.

"Was not!" said Hattie. She gave him a little push. Edward pushed her back. The push sent her tooth flying out of her mouth again. It landed in Mary Ellen's curly hair.

"Ow. Quit that!" she said as Hattie tried to pull it out.

"Stand still," said the photographer.

Hattie's tooth dropped from Mary Ellen's

hair to the ground. Then it bounced down the steps. Hattie bent down to find it.

"One—two—three—*cheese!*"

But instead of saying *cheese*, Hattie started to fall and landed on Mary Ellen.

Mary Ellen started to fall and grabbed the children beside her. Everybody grabbed everybody else until the whole class fell down in a heap.

When the class picture was sent home, there was no Hattie in it.

"I don't see you, dear," said her mother.

"I didn't want to spoil the picture with my tooth missing," said Hattie. What she did not say was that she had to stand in the corner when the picture was taken!

ABOUT THE AUTHOR

Janet Quin-Harkin was born in England and attended school in Vienna and West Germany before receiving a B.A. from the University of London. Her two great interests have always been writing and the theater. She wrote her first poem at the age of four and later studied dance and drama. Eventually she settled for working in radio drama and later writing her own plays. Her first book for children, *Peter Penny's Dance,* was chosen by both *The New York Times* and *School Library Journal* as one of the Best Books of 1976. Currently she lives in California with her husband and four children.

ABOUT THE ARTIST

Susanna Natti was born in Gloucester, Massachusetts. From the time she was eight, she knew that she wanted to be an illustrator, and she was only ten when she began studying figure drawing. Her mother, Lee Kingman, a well-known children's book author, taught her that books are special, and her father encouraged the use of humor, which characterizes her drawings to this day. After receiving a B.A. in art history at Smith College, she attended both the Montserrat School of Visual Art and the Rhode Island School of Design. The first book she illustrated for children was published in 1978, and she now has more than fifteen books to her credit. She lives in Arlington, Massachusetts, with her husband, who is a professor at M.I.T.